HEART OF THE ARCTIC

The Story of a Polar Bear Family

SMITHSONIAN
WILD HERITAGE COLLECTION

To David,
my buddy and partner in life
— D. H.

Copyright © 1994 by Trudy Management Corporation,
165 Water Street, Norwalk, CT 06856 and the Smithsonian Institution,
Washington, DC 20560.

Soundprints is a Division of Trudy Management Corporation, Norwalk, Connecticut.

Book Design: Shields & Partners, Westport, CT

First Edition
10 9 8 7 6 5 4 3 2 1
Printed in Singapore

Acknowledgements:
    Our very special thanks to Dr. Charles Handley of the department of
vertebrate zoology at the Smithsonian's National Museum of Natural History
for his curatorial review.

Library of Congress Cataloging-in-Publication Data

Howland, Deborah.

Heart of the Arctic : the story of a polar bear family / by Deborah Howland.
        p.   cm.
Summary: A mother polar bear gives birth to two cubs under the frozen
tundra and cares for them until the next winter, teaching them to survive
on their own.
        ISBN 1-56899-064-2
1. Polar bear — Juvenile fiction. [1. Polar bear — Fiction.
2. Bears — Fiction.] I. Title.
        PZ10.3.H834He 1994   94-7583
        (E) — dc20   CIP
                                                                  AC

HEART OF THE ARCTIC

The Story of a Polar Bear Family

Deborah Howland

Soundprints
Where Children Discover Nature

It is December, heart of the long Arctic night. Weeks ago, Polar Bear Mother pushed the last bit of snow into place, sealing her den against the furious cold outside. It is just like her mother's snug home, where she was born five winters ago.

Nestled deep under the tundra ice, Mother gives birth to two cubs. The he-cub, White Bear, is a little larger than his creamy sister, Ivory Bear. Mother holds her tiny babies close to the heat of her body, never exposing them to the danger of the cold ice. The twins nurse on her rich milk, and grow quickly.

One day something wiggling on the ice next to Mother startles her from a nap. Ivory Bear sleeps peacefully tucked under Mother's arm, but White Bear has squirmed from her protection onto the deadly ice.

With a quick sweep of her huge paw, she scoops White Bear back into the warmth of her fur. Mother will be busy now that her cubs can crawl.

utside, the frozen tundra is calm and quiet. But not inside the den! White Bear and Ivory Bear have grown old enough to wrestle. They tumble off Mother's shaggy back to the icy floor. Brrr, it's cold! Growling and nipping, they roll all around. The den is too crowded for Mother. She is tired and hungry from months without food. She longs for the spring hunt.

A coat of yellow sun soon lies upon the ice and snow. Mother senses the beginning of the spring thaw. Slowly, wearily, she digs out the snow-blocked entrance.

Brilliant sunlight explodes through the entryway. It sends Ivory Bear and White Bear scurrying back to the darkness of the den. Mother gently beckons them forward, into a huge and frightening new world.

But Mother isn't frightened. She's hungry! After a satisfying first meal of willow leaves and frozen berries, Mother leads her cubs home to the nearby den.

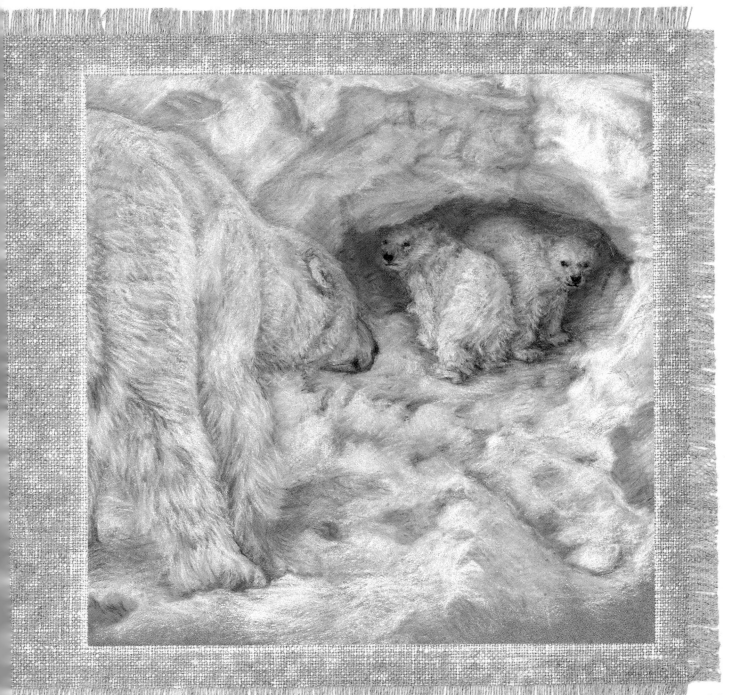

On days when the sun glints playfully over the tundra, Mother forages for food while the cubs explore. What are those hard, gray mounds peeking through the snow? Who's that baby bear reflected in a puddle of melted ice?

Ivory Bear sniffs a lemming as it races to a new patch of snow...one nip of its sharp little teeth and... she zips back to Mother.

Mother and the cubs settle into a peaceful rhythm of travelling back and forth between the wonders of the tundra and the familiar den. Yet as spring begins to soften the Arctic, Mother feels a growing restlessness.

Plants taste good, but seal is a polar bear's favorite food. Mother knows the time has come to leave the winter den and journey to their yearly hunting grounds amid the drifting ice. They begin the long trek — with White Bear and Ivory Bear stepping in Mother's tracks.

Grrr! Ivory Bear cries for help. She is stuck in Mother's deep footprint! Patiently, Mother lifts her by the scruff of her neck and places the cub on the unbroken snow beside her.

Trudging through snow is hard work for two young bears. Mother rests the cubs often, even though she is feeling well-fed and full of energy.

One day, Mother climbs to the top of a rise, then tucks and rolls. The youngsters, thrilled by Mother's wonderful new game, flop and sprawl down the hill after her.

Mother urges them on by day. At night they sleep beneath dancing northern lights. Mother and the cubs reach the coast and march northward along its ice-locked shore.

A scent drifts in on the wind. Seal! Just what they need to fatten themselves after the long unforgiving winter.

Mother guides the cubs over the frozen ocean to the water's edge. Blue-white ice floes rise up from the sea. They have arrived at the birthwaters of the ringed seal.

Always alert, Mother realizes that she and her cubs are not the only new arrivals on the ice.

Nose quivering, Mother catches the scent of danger. She wheels around, face to face with two fierce wolves. Ivory Bear and White Bear huddle fearfully behind her. One wolf snaps at Mother's paws, hoping she will leave her small cubs an unprotected easy catch for his wolf partner.

21

Mother sees no place to hide. With a growl, she pushes her cubs into the chilly waters and dives in after them. Grabbing them with her mouth, Mother flings the surprised cubs onto her back. She strokes the water with her powerful front paws, leaving the wolves far behind.

For three months the bears hunt seals and ride the drifting ice floes. There is so much here for a young polar bear to learn. A black nose stands out against the white Arctic. Keeping it buried beneath a clump of snow hides it from seals. Successful hunters ease backward quietly into the water. Graceful dives are noisy and should be saved for swim practice!

The warmth and sunlit nights of Arctic summer fade quickly. Shorter days and black nights mark the onset of fall. Winds blow the floating ice southward, returning Mother and her cubs to the ice-locked shore. They retrace their original route to their old home on the tundra. It looks so different! Much snow has melted and dried flowers curl their petals against the chilly air.

The bears pass the first few weeks browsing on frosty grasses and berries. One day, Mother hears a slurping sound. She discovers two purple-faced youngsters sitting in a berry patch.

A month later, the little berry bushes again lie blanketed beneath drifting snow. The bears ready their old den for another winter. They eat and grow very fat, until biting winds drive them into the waiting den. Mother and the cubs settle down to spend their last months together.

When spring arrives, Mother must leave them to start a new family. The cubs repeat last year's journey to the ice floes. But as the season turns wintery, White Bear strikes off to hunt by himself. His sister returns to the tundra to build a home all her own.

Ivory Bear is alone. She pushes the last bit of snow into place, sealing her den against the furious cold outside. It is just like Mother's snug home where she was born two winters ago.

About the Polar Bear

Polar bears are among the world's largest meat-eating land animals. While cubs only weigh about one and a half pounds at birth, adult females range from 400 to 650 pounds and males up to 1750 pounds when fully grown. A polar bear's greatest challenge is to survive the -30°F or more Arctic cold. But, a polar bear is well adapted. An extra membrane over its eyes protects against the intense glare of the sun. Broad feet bottomed with fur and rough black pads allow travel across the ice.

Polar bears appear to have white fur because their coat of thick colorless hair reflects light. However, some are hollow "guard" hairs that trap ultraviolet light to provide extra warmth. Polar bears also have black skin to soak in the warmth from the sun and a layer of fat up to four inches thick.

Since polar bear cubs are not so well adapted for the bitter Arctic, mothers are ever watchful. When the cubs are old enough to travel, a mother uses her body to shield them during bad weather and cold nights. Polar bear mothers are considered to be among the most affectionate of all mothers in the animal world.

Glossary

Arctic: The area in which no trees can grow extending down from the North Pole to approximately 65°N latitude.

den: A cave-like home that a polar bear digs ten or more feet under the drifting ice and snow.

drifting ice (or ice floes): Large pieces of ice and snow that form when solid ice covering the ocean begins to thaw and break apart.

lemming: A small rodent that digs tunnels running under the surface of the snow.

long Arctic night: The period when the sun remains below the horizon 24 hours a day during winter.

northern lights (or aurora borealis): The lights in the Arctic sky seen during early spring and late fall caused by the interaction between the earth's atmosphere and floating particles from the sun. They resemble a curtain of white, yellow and pink light.

ringed seals: The smallest of the seals. They make up the largest portion of a polar bear's diet.

sunlit nights: The period when the sun remains above the horizon 24 hours a day during late spring and summer.

tundra: Regions with low temperatures and permanently frozen subsoil.

Points of Interest in this Book

pp. 16-17 Arctic fox.

pp. 26-27 Arctic poppies, lichens.

pp. 28-29 long-tailed jaegar (left), raven (center), glaucous gull (right).